On Friday Afternoon

To S (who once broke his baby toe while vacuuming on a Friday afternoon, but still made sure everything was clean before sitting down). You're my favoritest.
—M. B.

PJ Library special edition 2024
Text copyright ©2024 by Michal Babay
Illustrations copyright ©2024 by Menahem Halberstadt
All rights reserved, including the right of reproduction in whole or in part in any form.
Charlesbridge and colophon are registered trademarks of Charlesbridge Publishing, Inc.

At the time of publication, all URLs printed in this book were accurate and active. Charlesbridge, the author, and the illustrator are not responsible for the content or accessibility of any website.

Published by Charlesbridge
9 Galen Street
Watertown, MA 02472
(617) 926-0329
www.charlesbridge.com

Library of Congress Cataloging-in-Publication Data
Names: Babay, Michal, author. | Halberstadt, Menahem, illustrator.
Title: On Friday afternoon / Michal Babay; illustrated by Menahem Halberstadt.
Description: Watertown, MA: Charlesbridge Publishing, [2024] | Audience: Ages 5–8. | Audience: Grades K–1. | Summary: Leelee and her dog perform mitzvahs around the house to get ready for Shabbat.
Identifiers: LCCN 2021052933 (print) | LCCN 2021052934 (ebook) | ISBN 9781623543570 (hardcover) | ISBN 9781632893291 (ebook)
Subjects: LCSH: Jewish children—Juvenile fiction. | Sabbath—Juvenile fiction. | Commandments (Judaism)—Juvenile fiction. | CYAC: Jews—Fiction. | Sabbath—Fiction. | Commandments (Judaism)—Fiction. | LCGFT: Picture books. | Fiction.
Classification: LCC PZ7.1.B116 On 2024 (print) | LCC PZ7.1.B116 (ebook) | DDC [E]—dc23
LC record available at https://lccn.loc.gov/2021052933
LC ebook record available at https://lccn.loc.gov/2021052934

Printed in China
(hc) 10 9 8 7 6 5 4 3 2 1
(pb) 10 9 8 7 6 5 4 3 2 1

Illustrations created digitally
Display and text type set in Grenadine by Akemi Aoki
Printed by 1010 Printing International Limited in Huizhou, Guangdong, China
Production supervision by Nicole Turner
Designed by Kristen Nobles
1024/B2707/A4

On Friday Afternoon

A SHABBAT CELEBRATION

Michal Babay

Illustrated by **Menahem Halberstadt**

Charlesbridge

On Friday afternoon,
while chicken soup bubbles and apple tarts bake,

Leelee and Pickles grab one
(or two)
(or three)
warm challahs to taste-test together...

then giggle and chomp
as they race through the house,
trailing crumbs over Dad's
freshly vacuumed rugs.

But Shabbat starts in three hours,
and the house needs to be clean.

So they quickly pick up
(and lick up) each crumb.
Which means . . .

Leelee and Pickles discover
eight quarters, six pennies, and a sock
under the couch.

Perfect for Friday tzedakah!

They want to donate their treasure,
but every container is full.

So Pickles unearths a new one.

They replant the flowers
and decorate their new tzedakah box.

In goes all their loot:

Clink! Clink! Squish!

That was such fun. So they look for more things to donate.

Leelee zips through her drawers, grabbing clothes she's outgrown.

Along the way Leelee and Pickles find an old friend. And a new hat!

Hard work makes them thirsty.
So they run to the kitchen for a cold drink.
Which means . . .

Crash!

they end up grapey and soaked.

Only two hours till candle lighting!
So they quickly mop up
(and slurp up)
everything sticky.

Well . . . not everything.

Cleaning reminds them it's time for *their* bath
(Pickles's least favorite Friday mitzvah).
So they fill up the bathtub with oodles of suds.

Leelee and Pickles dry off, then deck themselves out in
splendid Shabbat outfits. But . . .

Leelee's sparkly left shoe has disappeared!
They search everywhere. Which means ...

they also discover Mom's car keys,
one green earring, and a long-lost trombone.

Pah! Bah-bah! Rah!

They parade through the house to
return things to Mom,
but a procession of two is too small.

So Leelee and Pickles invite
family and friends,
who come and join in the fun.

And of course Leelee and Pickles invite everyone over for dinner.

But now there are only ten minutes
until candle lighting. Which means . . .

it's all hands on deck!

Dad picks up every heap, stack, and pile.

Pickles picks up every shoe.

A cousin adds flavorful food to the table.
Leelee adds fabulous flair.

Friends dig up extra chairs, plates, and glasses.
Pickles digs up extra treats.

Mom watches over the roast and the kugel,
and everyone watches the clock.

Until *finally*...

Shabbat Shalom.

On Friday night,
while candlelight flickers and everyone talks,
Leelee, Pickles, and Grandma grab one
(or two)
(or three)

apple tarts to taste-test during dinner . . .
and to share with all of their family and friends.

AUTHOR'S NOTE

The literal meaning of the Hebrew word *mitzvah* is "commandment," but it is commonly understood to mean a good deed or charitable act. Although there are 613 mitzvahs in Judaism, they come in all shapes and sizes for every member of the family. Jews believe in tikkun olam, which means "to do something with the world that will not only fix any damage, but also improve upon it" (Chabad.org).

In order to improve the world around you, here are a few mitzvahs you can do alone or with your family:

1. Donate money, clothes, and toys to those in need (tzedakah).

2. Collect groceries for a food bank (ha'achalat re'evim).

3. Return lost objects to the rightful owner (hashavat aveidah).

4. Visit a sick friend or elderly person (bikur cholim).

5. Keep yourself clean and healthy (shmirat haguf).

6. Apologize if you've done something wrong, and find a way to repair the damage (teshuvah).

7. Welcome guests into your home and your life (hachnasat orchim).

8. Speak kindly about others and avoid gossip (lashon hara).

9. Be kind to animals. Feed your pets before feeding yourself (tza'ar ba'alei hayim).

10. Take care of the environment (bal tashchit).

11. Respect your parents (kibbud av v'eim).

12. Help clean your house, prepare dinner, and set the table for Shabbat (kavod shabbat).

Shabbat, the twenty-five hours beginning at sundown on Friday evening and lasting until three stars appear on Saturday night, is a special part of the week in Judaism. Following the commandment to "remember" and to "guard" (zachor and shamor), Shabbat instructs us to set aside this time as a special period of rest and reflection. Jewish families traditionally spend this time praying, playing games, and eating long meals together.

To prepare for this important part of the week, we cook special meals and make sure everything (and everyone!) is clean. Many families give extra tzedakah before lighting the candles.

This is all done so that we may welcome Shabbat into our homes joyously and with the same respect we'd give an honored guest.